To Thomas
The hero of the story!

Thomas Panda and his friends are playing their best-loved game of roly poly.

It is lots of fun and much better than walking.

4

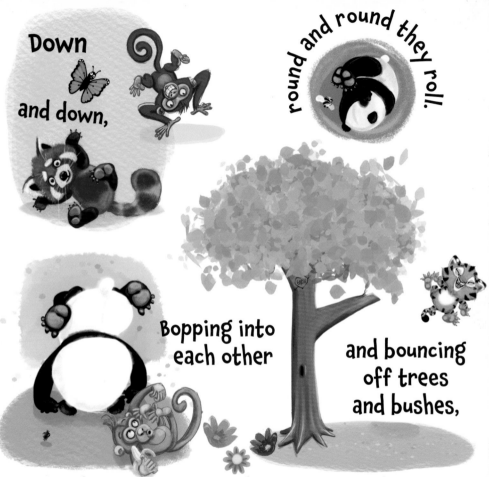

Down
and down,

round and round they roll.

Bopping into
each other

and bouncing
off trees
and bushes,

Pandas are so fluffy they never get hurt.

5

Suddenly –

SPLASH

they roll into an unexpected puddle of water.
Where has it come from? It hasn't been raining!

As they shake the water from their fur,

Thomas can see that the nearby river has burst its banks and he wonders why.

7

Thomas looks downstream and notices that the river is blocked with plastic bottles and other rubbish.

"Oh no!" exclaims Thomas "the water can't get through."

8

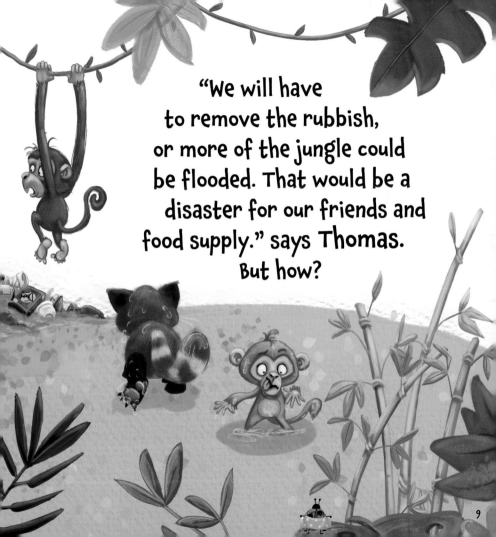

"We will have to remove the rubbish, or more of the jungle could be flooded. That would be a disaster for our friends and food supply." says Thomas. But how?

Thomas looks around
and sees his friend
Tumble is eating
some bamboo...

...and this
gives him
an idea.

10

Thomas asks Tumble to chomp down two long lengths of bamboo,

while he tears off strips from another piece and cleverly twists the strips into a net.

11

Working together the friends make an amazing makeshift bridge.

They wonder how to get it across the water.

"I know" says the tallest stretchiest monkey, waggling his floppy hands, "I can swing across!"

Using an extra long vine and taking an extra big leap...

12

...the monkey swings safely to the other side, landing like an acrobat.

Bit by bit, Thomas and his friends push the bamboo bridge across to him. The monkey stretches out his long arms and grabs the bridge, then using some vines he ties the bamboo bridge tightly to a nearby tree.

Thomas carefully shimmies out onto the bridge. Being a bear, he's not scared of climbing.

Just as he reaches the middle he loses his grip and starts to slip!

Luckily he manages to hang on with his strong legs and sharp claws. Dangling upside down, he sees that he is close to the rubbish swirling in the water below.

Clinging on to the bridge, Thomas begins scooping up the nasty rubbish with the net.

The other jungle creatures all want to help, so Thomas passes the rubbish filled net to a monkey...

...who then gives it to the red panda...

...who finally hands it to the tiger!

The tiger empties the rubbish into one big pile.
"Why don't we call ourselves the Eco Crew,
as we are doing such a good job."
says the tiger. "That is a great idea."
says Thomas.

Finally, the last piece of rubbish is collected...

...and the river runs freely again. HOORAY!

Tumble the red panda asks where the rubbish came from.

Thomas explains that instead of recycling it,

some people just throw their rubbish on the ground and a lot of it ends up in rivers and even in the SEA!

"That is terrible," says the red panda.
"We should remind everyone that -
If everybody does their bit
the planet will be fighting fit."

Thomas and the Eco Crew stand in front of the big pile of rubbish, happy with doing their bit to help.

The end